HOW TO GET RICH ON A TEXAS CATTLE DRIVE

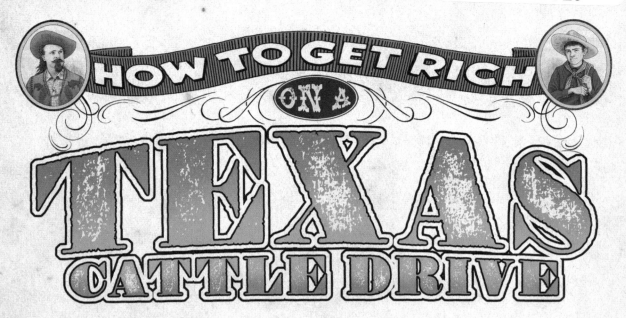

NATIONAL GEOGRAPHIC

WASHINGTON, D.C.

This never-before-published narrative of one cowboy's life on the trail and stage stands as an invaluable contribution to the literature of the western frontier. Written at the close of the 19th century, it came to light only recently upon the death of the author's grandson, Walter Larken. Mr. Larken, who built a worldwide entertainment empire around the popular theme park WestWorld, was tragically trampled to death in a stampede while inspecting his WestWorld Wild Bison Shooting Range.

The theme-park magnate apparently did not think much of his grandfather's literary talents. Mr. Larken's daughter found the manuscript at her father's 480,000-acre Montana ranch, lining the cages of Mr. Larken's 87 pet prairie dogs. After painstaking labor, the pages were recovered with minimal soiling. Scholars of Western history and the reading public alike will be thrilled to find the lively text and vivid illustrations reproduced in this instructive and entertaining volume.

William "Big Bill" Crawford,
PhD, Professor of Rodeo Sciences,
Lost Frontier University (L.F.U.)

Editor's note: Professor Crawford's claims notwithstanding, the Larken family have left no trace of their existence in the historical record, outside the pages of this manuscript. While the book gives a reliable picture of life on the cattle trail and can be read for its tremendous educational value, we cannot vouch for its accuracy in all matters, nor can we be held responsible for any fun sustained while reading.

A TYPICAL COWHAND IN ALL HIS GLORY

bandana for blocking out the dust, drying dishes, tying a hat on, or straining the mud out of your drinking water

Stetson to fan the fire, carry water, or keep your hair looking fine for the ladies

Bull Durham *tobacco*

gloves to keep hands from bleeding on your horse

rope for tying ornery steer, corraling horses, or hanging horse thieves

good *buckskin chaps* to protect your lone pair of pants

CONTENTS

Why I Was
Born to Be a Cowboy

SINCE **I** WAS **LITTLE** there's only been two things important to me: horses and trains. Well, make it three on account of money ought to be in there too. Still, I was in a saddle before I could count pennies, and I spent so many hours on a horse's back that I never did learn to walk so good. That is one thing I can't blame on my parents, who tried to keep my feet on the ground and my backside in school. But even at a tender age I had a headstrong streak in me wide as a prairie dust cloud.

I reckon with all of these things put together, I never had a choice but to try my hand as a cowboy. And that is as it must be, because no one would freely choose to spend his days half starved, shot at, deprived of sleep, choked with dirt, and near trampled by half-ton beasts. I feel it my duty to warn any children unlucky enough to have happened across this account of my life and adventures: Do not be blinded by the hard-driving excitement, the breath-catching suspense, and the romance of this tale. Learn your sums and letters, and keep your hindquarters out of the saddle.

Here is the **hero of my youth**, a showman, scout, expert hunter, and a major player in the story of my life. And that is all I'm telling of him, until he appears again in these pages.

To Chicago

BIRDS EYE VIEW OF THE CITY OF

CEDAR RAPIDS.

LINN CO. KINGSTON IOWA 1868.

Cedar River

My daddy worked here, in the Sinclair meat-packing factory, making hogs into canned dinner for city folk in the east.

No train could match me and Prince (who was named after Buffalo Bill's first horse)—leastways in the first 200 yards.

The Trail Calls
and
I Answer

I LIT OUT WHEN I WAS knee-high to a prairie dog. That's merely a way of saying I was still a boy—just shy of 16 years—because I never been knee-high to anything. Long as I can remember I been tall as a stalk of corn, which is why they call me Little John. And if that seems like a sensible thing to you, you are probably made right for the life of a cowhand.

Anyway, when I left, my daddy tried to stop me, but I told him, "Daddy, a boy my size can't hardly stretch his legs in a town like this. There is open land out there, and I need to be riding it." Daddy never did have a leaning toward the poetic side of life, but I told him my plan was to ride just till I had money enough to buy my own herd and earn my living as a rancher. When I went over the considerable fortune to be made on the range, he softened right up. And for any greenhorns who might be reading this tract, I'll present on this page a lesson in the moneymaking potential of the cattle trade.

In Texas, 15 years before the day I said fare-thee-well to my home, there were **more cattle than people**. Millions of them roamed free, just waiting for a rancher to round them up and claim them as his own.

But that cozy situation was exactly the problem. There were so many cattle and so few people to buy them that you couldn't get but four lousy dollars for a 1,000-pound steer.

Then a rancher named **Charlie Goodnight** come along, and he must have been smarter than Thomas Alva Edison. He had an idea to make himself a raise of money.

GOODNIGHT'S PLAN

1 **Trail the cattle** up north to Kansas where the rail lines run east.

2 **Load them** on boxcars and collect $40—not $4—a head.

3 Send them to **Chicago** or **Philadelphia** or **New York** where they end their days as a dinner of steak and onions for a gentleman of means.

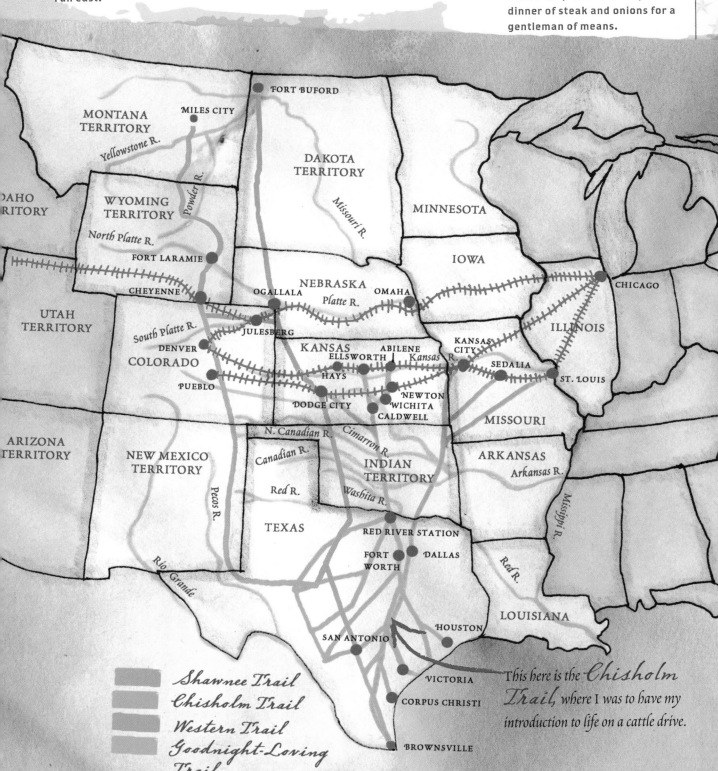

MONTANA TERRITORY

MILES CITY

FORT BUFORD

DAKOTA TERRITORY

MINNESOTA

Yellowstone R.

Powder R.

IDAHO RITORY

WYOMING TERRITORY

North Platte R.

FORT LARAMIE

Missouri R.

IOWA

CHEYENNE

OGALLALA

NEBRASKA

Platte R.

OMAHA

CHICAGO

UTAH TERRITORY

South Platte R.

JULESBERG

DENVER

COLORADO

PUEBLO

KANSAS

ELLSWORTH

HAYS

DODGE CITY

ABILENE

Kansas

NEWTON

WICHITA

CALDWELL

KANSAS CITY

Kansas R.

SEDALIA

ST. LOUIS

ILLINOIS

MISSOURI

ARIZONA TERRITORY

NEW MEXICO TERRITORY

N. Canadian R.

Canadian R.

Cimarron R.

INDIAN TERRITORY

ARKANSAS

Arkansas R.

Red R.

Washita R.

Pecos R.

TEXAS

RED RIVER STATION

FORT WORTH

DALLAS

Red R.

Mississippi R.

Río Grande

SAN ANTONIO

HOUSTON

LOUISIANA

VICTORIA

CORPUS CHRISTI

BROWNSVILLE

Shawnee Trail
Chisholm Trail
Western Trail
Goodnight-Loving Trail

This here is the Chisholm Trail, where I was to have my introduction to life on a cattle drive.

I Wrestle an "Alligator"
and Join an Outfit

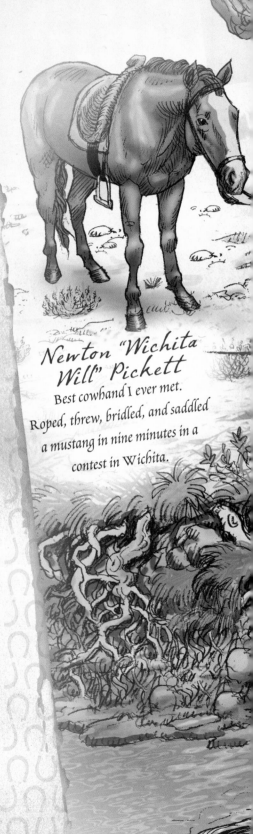

Newton "Wichita Will" Pickett
Best cowhand I ever met.
Roped, threw, bridled, and saddled
a mustang in nine minutes in a
contest in Wichita.

I **BADE MY PARENTS GOODBYE** in the summer, it being 1877. I was a little light in the pocket, but I had Prince, a fine saddle, a sturdy pair of boots, and my rifle so I wouldn't get lonesome. Considerable wealth was surely in store, and no one could have told me otherwise.

Me and Prince were deep into Kansas when I found what I was looking for. I was catching forty winks on the banks of the Cimarron River when I had a rude awakening. I heard a splash, and a voice yelled out "Alligator!" inches from my ear. I wasn't the scaring kind, but when I saw something long and dark in the water below, I scrambled for my life. The bank being muddy, I went feet up and slid right into the river toward the jaws of a hungry beast.

Well, the "alligator" turned out to be a log thrown in the water by the sorriest band of prankster cowhands you ever saw. As I came up from the river, they stood laughing on the bank. I wrung myself out, straightened up tall, pointed to the log, and said, "Anyone else care to wrestle, you'll end up as dead as that alligator down there." And that was my introduction to the men who would be my companions, for better or worse, for the next year.

These boys were a sight! They were on their way back from a trail drive and they had freshened up in Dodge City. But a hog in a silk waistcoat, boys and girls, is still a hog.

Billy "Kid" Barnes
Being the youngest in the outfit, Billy and me looked out for one another.

Amos "Grizzly" Clay
Our foreman. Mean as a hungry bear.

Hector "Guts" Amado
Our cook.

LEDGER		July 1877
BEGINNING BALANCE	*It took some convincing, but my daddy made me a loan to get me to Texas.*	$20
INCOME		0
EXPENSES		
	Missouri River ferry	$.50
	dinner (Omaha)	$2
	trail food (biscuits, dried beef)	$3
CURRENT BALANCE		$14.50
DEBT		$20

We Encounter
a Migration of Indians

IT WAS JULY, I reckon, and hotter than Hades when we came upon the most curious sight I have had the privilege to witness. Just over the Cimarron, in Indian Territory, was a line of Indians stretched out far as I could see. It must have been a mile long and comprising nearly a thousand people—braves and squaws and children alike. Riding in front and behind and alongside like cowhands managing a herd were almost a hundred cavalrymen, all buttoned up in their blue coats. Grizzly Clay went to have a word with the commander, a tower of a man by the name of Lawton, whom the Indians called Tall White Man.

Turns out it was a solemn procession of Cheyenne come down from Fort Robinson in Nebraska. Along with the Sioux, they had surrendered in the spring at the end of the Black Hills War. With nowhere left to go, they agreed to leave their hunting grounds and live with the other tribes in Indian Territory. They didn't look too happy about it, but with all that hardware around them, I don't imagine they complained too much. Leastways not till later, when they will make a return to our story.

The Black Hills War started when prospectors found gold in the Black Hills of Dakota. Pretty soon the army wanted the Sioux and the Cheyenne out of them hills to make room for gold hunters.

CUSTER'S LAST CHARGE

Custer's Todes-Ritt.

Colonel George Armstrong Custer went after the Black Hills Indians, who were laying for him along the Little Big Horn River. His men were wiped out. But in the end it was no use for the Indians. They might as well have taken on a swarm of locusts as tried to fight off a horde of gold-hungry men.

Here is **Sitting Bull**, chief of the Hunkpapa Sioux, who refused to surrender and went to Canada, saying he would die before he came back.

I am part Indian myself, which is a thing not many people know. My great-grandaddy trapped for furs in the Dakotas, and the story goes that he met an Indian maiden while chasing a bear one day and made her his bride. Her name was Mikama, which means "butterfly" in the Cheyenne language, and this is what I imagine she looked like.

RUNNING ROOSTER RANCH
SEPTEMBER 1877

My new home in the south of Texas,
as best I can render it.

Mr. Shanghai Morse was the owner of this fine establishment. Word has it he came west from Rhode Island on account of he felt too fenced in.

Here is the cookshack, where Guts did the work of the Devil.

This here is the blacksmith shop, where the mustangs got their proper footwear.

We called Mr. Amos Clay's place the Bear's Lair. He liked to shoot prairie dogs from his doorway at dawn, and woe to the person who got in the way.

There were no feather beds in our bunkhouse, but a straw mat is a downy paradise to a man whose backside has felt nothing but hard leather since sunup.

The corral was to be my domain, for I was hired as wrangler to look after the horse herd, known in cowboy parlance as the remuda.

LEDGER

BEGINNING BALANCE		$14.50
INCOME	Mr. Morse offered me $25 a month wages and took me to San Antonio to outfit me properly. When I thanked him, he told me to save my breath; I would be thanking him with my first two-and-a-half months' wages.	$0.00
EXPENSES		
	PAID BY SHANGHAI	
	pistol (Colt 45)	$12.00
	spurs	$8.00
	Stetson "conk cover"	$10.00
	chaps	$5.00
	saddlebags (less trade of old saddlebags)	$26.00
	PAID BY ME	
	Beadle's dime novels (20 brand new)	$2.00
	Bull Durham tobacco	$2.25
CURRENT BALANCE		$10.25
DEBT		
	Shanghai	$61.00
	Daddy	$20.00

I Am Tested and Pass
With Bruises to Show for It

ONE THING ABOUT A COWBOY is he don't take kindly to fools, city folk, or greenhorns who can't tell the front end of a horse from the back. Every new hand gets a test, and mine came early on. The boys had rounded up a herd of mustangs, fresh from their freedom on the range and none too happy to be surrounded by animals of the two-legged variety. One horse in particular, a big brown stallion, looked ready to break the neck of any fool that tried to mount it. Even Will

flat out refused to go near it. But Grizzly said to me, "If you can bust a gator, boy, surely you can do as well with a horse." In front of all the hands he laid out $5 if I could stay on that horse's back for half a minute. If I got thrown, I had to work as Guts's washup boy for the rest of the month. Bets were still being placed when I snuck up on that pony and climbed aboard for a ride on the hurricane deck. I lasted exactly 32 seconds before making a hard landing in the dirt. Grizzly, who was a regular old sore head, had it in for me from the moment I took those five shiny dollar pieces out of his hand.

How to Break a Wild Horse

MR. SHANGHAI MORSE,

LIKE MANY RANCHERS,

PAID A PROFESSIONAL TO DO IT. These fellows earn **$5** a mustang, ᴀɴᴅ *I considered myself fully qualified to do the same.*

FIRST, the bronc gets roped, bridled, and cross-hobbled if need be.

NEXT comes 40 pounds' worth of saddle and 160 pounds of rider. A painful tweak of the ear helps keep the bronc's mind off the business at hand.

THEN THE FUN BEGINS.

A good rider stays up till the horse is ready to drop. Then he does it the next day and the next till the horse is broke.

I Learn
the Tricks
of the Trade
on Roundup

IN MY LIFE I have met men who are rich and men who are honest, but few men who are both at the same time. Mr. Shanghai Morse was no exception to that rule.

In February he sent me and 15 other hands to cut out a herd to drive to market. In those days, ranchers and farmers were starting to fence in the land to claim their own piece of ground. But the cattle were still able to mingle on the range, and it was our job on roundup to determine which of the beasts belonged to us. First we had to find our own brand and cut out the four-year-olds that were ready for the supper table. Then we had to cut out the new calves and brand them.

Old Shanghai gave out two more jobs of a less savory type. We were to bring in as many mavericks as we could and give them our own brand. The second job became clear when I found Grizzly and a couple of old hands cutting out the cattle of Mr. K. P. Parker and "blotching" the brand to make it look like ours. When I have my own ranch, I thought to myself, I will use an uncommon method known as honest hard work.

HOW TO BLOTCH A BRAND

EXPERT ADVICE FROM AN ARTFUL VETERAN, MR. GRIZZLY CLAY.

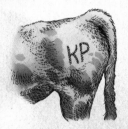

☞ Round up a couple thousand head with Mr. K. P. Parker's brand.

☞ Apply a useful straight-edged tool known as a running iron.

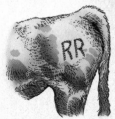

☞ Report to your boss that his Running Rooster brand has mysteriously increased by 1,800 over the winter.

It could take *three hands* to brand one strong=minded calf.

Colorado Branding Calves

This here is **Mr. Samuel Maverick.** In 1847, he took a herd of 400 head as payment for a debt. They went unbranded and untended for so long that when they strayed into another rancher's land, people started saying, "Yonder goes a 'maverick.'"

LEDGER

September 1877–January 1878

BEGINNING BALANCE	
INCOME	$10.25
5 months' wages	$125
wager with Grizzly	$5
EXPENSES	
Shanghai loan (with 5% interest monthly)	$78.50
pants (riveted)	$5
overshirt (embroidered)	$7
fine woolen coat and vest	$38
Beadles	$2
CURRENT BALANCE	
DEBT	$9.75
Daddy	$20

I will own up to a weakness for the clothiers of San Antone.

I Am Broken In
by Life on the Trail

COME JUNE we were fed up with ranch life and hankering to get on the trail. Shanghai had hired 15 of us to trail 5,000 head of cattle, 800 of them headed for Indian Territory, 2,000 for Wyoming, and the rest to the railhead in Kansas. I had in my charge a herd of 120 mustangs, which gave each cowhand eight horses to wear out in four months on the trail. It was my job to get each of my grateful compatriots a fresh mount every four hours or thereabouts.

But as rough as a horse has it on the trail, there is one creature has it harder, and that is a cowhand. In the event you do not believe me, here is a list of the hazards we met in the first week alone: A hailstorm so fierce it persuaded us to stop and hide under our saddles; rain that never let up all day and soaked through my saddlebags into my spare clothes; thunder that spooked the herd into a stampede, during which I rode all night, lost my hat, and got my saddle trampled in a nasty spill. I could write more but it would take up another book to tell the rest.

I was squalling to Billy about not sleeping for two days when Grizzly, who has ears like a coyote, heard me. "Quit your kicking!" he growled. "You can sleep all winter when you get back to Texas."

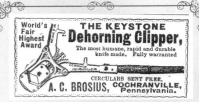
WAYS TO BREAK AN OUTLAW

THERE WERE SOME ORNERY BEEVES IN EVERY HERD THAT WERE JUST ITCHING TO LEAD A STAMPEDE, AND WE HAD TO SHOW EACH AND EVERY ONE WHO WAS BOSS.

- ☞ sew his eyelids shut; by the time the thread rots, he's tame as a kitten
- ☞ pierce his nose and put a rope through the hole
- ☞ chop his horns with an ax
- ☞ shoot him and hand him over to Guts
- ☞ rub tobacco juice in his eyes

How to Drive a Herd

A DAY IN THE LIFE OF A TRAIL-WORN CREW ON THE OLD PRAIRIE

THIS was the scene every morning after grub: Each cowhand ropes an unlucky steed out of the remuda for the day's work. Then they all take up their positions around the herd.

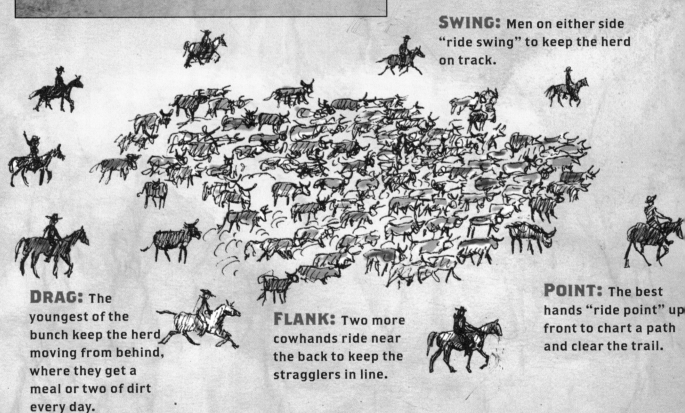

SWING: Men on either side "ride swing" to keep the herd on track.

DRAG: The youngest of the bunch keep the herd moving from behind, where they get a meal or two of dirt every day.

FLANK: Two more cowhands ride near the back to keep the stragglers in line.

POINT: The best hands "ride point" up front to chart a path and clear the trail.

AFTER a day in the saddle, the chuck wagon was our only relief. Sad to say there was no relief from the effects of the slop Guts liked to call grub.

I Make
My Debut
Performance
as a Trail Boss

IN JUNE we trailed the herd to Fort Worth, which was the westernmost station on the Texas-Pacific rail line. Being the last town of any account before Kansas, it was filled with stores and entertainments for the likes of us. Six thousand people made their home there, and they had taverns enough for 6,000 more.

We were met outside the town by salesmen from the outfitting establishments looking to gain the favor of the trail boss with a few friendly gifts. Old Grizzly was under a tree somewhere keeping up with his trail log, and I hated to see those hardworking fellows make the trip for nothing. So I pulled my hat low, stood up high, and went to make my introduction as the Top Screw. These

good businessmen, possessed of a skeptical nature, were a mite slow to believe that we had such a young trail boss. But, not wanting to risk putting the purchaser of the outfit in a bad humor, they freely handed over some fine cigars and bottles of whiskey.

Alas, my performance did not please all the critics. Grizzly arrived in the middle of it and sentenced me to scrubbing pots for the rest of the drive.

It took us three tries to find a place **willing to serve Will.** Grizzly grumbled plenty about having a damn Negro cowhand, but I took notice of the fact that he refused to drink till we could all lift a glass together.

Some of the good people of Fort Worth complained about us cowhands tearing up the town, but those who had found a way to take our money were most welcoming. At a place called the Headlight Bar we found this sign: *"Ride right in boys, and get bar service in the saddle."*

LEDGER

February–May 1878

BEGINNING BALANCE			$9.75
INCOME	*I made $30 a month for the drive but wasn't to see a cent till the end of the trail.*	4 months' wages	$100
EXPENSES		new hat	$12
		new saddle	$35
	I sent him double to show I was making something of myself	gambling losses (monte)	$15
		dining (Fort Worth)	$4.50
		loan payment (Daddy)	$40
CURRENT BALANCE			$3.25

N. Canadian R.

Cimarron R.

MEXICO TERRITORY

Canadian R.

INDIAN TERRITORY

Pecos R.

Red R.

Washita R.

TEXAS

Grande

Eighty miles up the trail from Fort Worth we came upon the **Red River**, which was tame as a kitten that year. It being the border of Texas, an inspector looked our herd up and down to make sure they all had our brand. Then he charged us four cents a head for his services.

23

We Prepare for Indian Attack
but Meet None

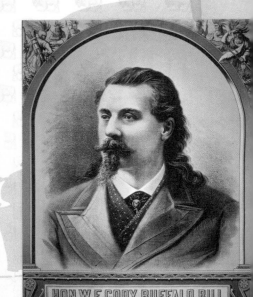

HON. W.F. CODY. BUFFALO BILL

I can barely describe my surprise and excitement upon seeing none other than my childhood hero, **Buffalo Bill**, at the agency. He had come to hire a band of Pawnees to perform in his new show. I made an introduction of myself and was interested to find he is hiring real cowboys as well.

HAVING CROSSED THE RED RIVER, we entered Indian Territory, and I found myself reflecting on the solemn procession of Cheyenne we saw last year. From here we had 300 miles of riding to Kansas, all of it belonging by treaty with Uncle Sam to the Indians. Sensible as we were of tales relating the depredations of the Red Man, we retrieved our Winchesters from the wagon and kept them at the ready on the saddle. And there they rested, for the people we saw, scattered about in small villages or begging beeves from us, were not the "savage foes" of Western lore but a sorry lot of starving human beings.

We met an old scout called Amos Chapman, who acted as interpreter for the Cheyenne. He said their people were getting beef, cornmeal, flour, sugar, and coffee, but no beans, rice, hard bread, or salt. Rations are issued for seven days but last only three. After months of pleading with the government agent, Cheyenne braves were allowed to go on a buffalo hunt, where they found nothing but bones left by white hunters.

By the time this picture was taken the *Cheyenne* were more or less resigned to living on the reservation. But when we went through, they were miserable as wild mustangs in a corral. A chief called Little Wolf complained that his people were dying every day and wanted to go back to their hunting grounds in the north. The government agent at the reservation, Mr. John D. Miles, flat out refused to let them go.

Grizzly had us cut out 800 of the scrawniest old cows to hand over to the **Indian agent**, for which Shanghai received a draft of **$15,200**. Not a bad income, considering no other soul would have paid a cent for mere skin and bones.

An old coot called *Stoppard*, who says he made and lost a fortune in Black Hills gold, hangs around the agency selling whiskey to the Indians. He says they are eager to buy it, and that there is yet another fortune to be made.

STAMPEDE ALONG THE CIMARRON RIVER
AUGUST 1878

A hand called *Jim* earned the name "Lucky" in this stampede. His leg was broke, and he was out of the drive, but the herd stepped lightly around his vital parts.

Some of the *other hands* pressed into the herd from the right to turn them.

One day as we got ready to cross into Kansas, the herd spooked and struck out for nowhere in a tempest of tails and horns.

Billy, who fell asleep on watch and couldn't say what caused the stampede, never did much but get caught in the wake.

Will got in front of the rampaging beeves, waving his slicker to get their attention, and I am pleased to say that I was right there alongside him. If only Buffalo Bill could have seen me.

No greenhorn will believe it, but the friction of a stampede can make a beef's horns flash blue.

The Cause of the Stampede
Is Discovered but Not Proved

BY **SUNUP** we had the herd quiet, but Grizzly was bellowing louder than a cow that's lost her calf. He reckoned we were out 400 head and a dollar off each of the others, seeing as a beef can lose 50 pounds on a four-hour run. It didn't help matters when several hard-looking citizens rode up and offered to bring in the lost beeves at $1 a head. It seemed plain that these were the fellows that stampeded the herd in the first place.

Billy, who was still smarting from his mistake the night before, started fingering his six-shooter and proposing to string them up. But Grizzly wasn't keen to do any lynching and didn't think it would get us our beeves back. He offered the scoundrels 50 cents a head instead, which they accepted right fast. We had half the missing animals back by sundown, and Grizzly thought it best to pay the men and be on our way.

When it came to rustlers, most cattlemen weren't as accommodating as Grizzly. They either fought to defend their herd or put up a reward so someone else would do the job. Rumor has it Shanghai once taught two brothers to brand mavericks for him. When the brothers started keeping some of the mavericks for themselves, old Shang hung them from a tree and made sure he tied the knot himself.

REWARD
($5,000)

REWARD FOR THE CAPTURE, DEAD OR ALIVE, OF ON PERCY E. WESTCREEK, BETTER KNOWN A

"The Tiger Bandit"

Age, 18, Height 5 feet, 8 inches. Weight, 145 lbs Brown hair, brown eyes, crooked features. He is the leader of the "Traveller Gang", the worst band of desperadoes the Territory has ever faced. The above reward will be paid for his capture.

Hal Luck, Sheriff.

Dead or Alive!

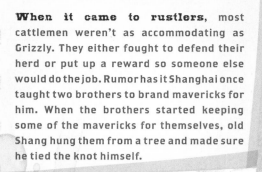

Some days later we found about **100 more of our cattle** by the Cimarron. Mad with thirst after the stampede, they must have met their end drinking alkali water.

In honor of my efforts during the stampede, Grizzly invited me to ride swing in "Lucky" Jim's place. I could hardly refuse, but it did not please Billy, who was forced to watch the remuda and take my place on washup duty.

We Meet the
Good Farmers of Kansas
and Are Treated as Trespassers

HAVING CROSSED THE CIMARRON, we struck west on account of the dirt farmers, who were settling the land by the thousands. They had already filled up Kansas to the east of the trail and had gotten the land closed off to Texas cattle. Can't say as I blame them, as 12,000 hooves can raze a crop of wheat quicker than a plague of locusts.

Grizzly, being a regular old sore head, was of a different mind. He went on about how he was trailing cattle up through Kansas way back when "them land-grubbing nesters" were still growing pumpkins in Pennsylvania.

But no matter what Grizzly thought, the Kansans had their way with us. When we came upon the lone watering hole between the Cimarron and Dodge City, we found it guarded by a posse of farmers carrying rifles instead of hoes. They claimed the land was theirs but they would let the cattle drink for the low price of ten cents a head. Grizzly was in a bad humor, but with the herd nearly dropping from thirst and one farmer waving a sheriff's badge, he reckoned a fight might cost him dearer than paying up.

The homesteaders built **sod houses** that were nothing but lumps in the ground. One of our lead steers got real curious about one and fell right through, which was most severe on the lady of the house. Grizzly made a gift of a fat cow in payment for the damage.

NEBRASKA

Platte R.

KANSAS

Kansas R.

DODGE CITY

N. Canadian R.

Cimarron R.

Canadian R.

INDIAN
TERRITORY

Settlers Taking the
Law in Their own hands
Cutting 15 Miles of the
Brighton Ranch fence in 1885
Copy Right By S.D. Butcher   Keatra, Neb.

What with farmers, rustlers, fences, and the like all conspiring against us, I was beginning to wonder whether trailing cattle held any promise for me. But with **Dodge City** and all of its enticements on the horizon, that was a concern for a later date.

Cattlemen didn't take kindly to the fences that were closing off trails and grazing land. Some cowhands found that a pair of **wire cutters** answered the problem most handily.

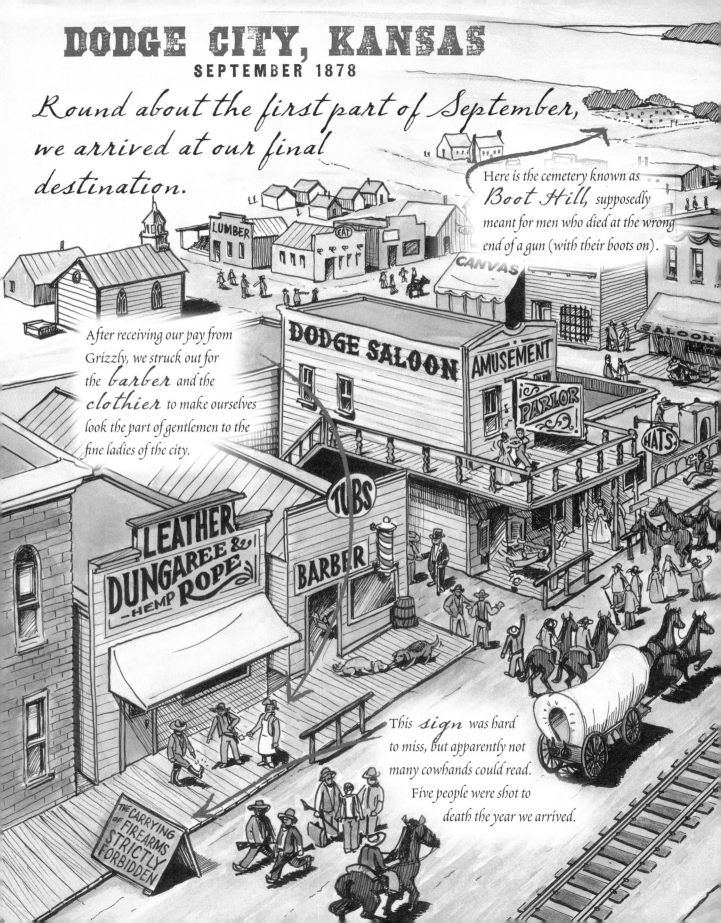

DODGE CITY, KANSAS
SEPTEMBER 1878

Round about the first part of September, we arrived at our final destination.

Here is the cemetery known as *Boot Hill,* supposedly meant for men who died at the wrong end of a gun (with their boots on).

After receiving our pay from Grizzly, we struck out for the *barber* and the *clothier* to make ourselves look the part of gentlemen to the fine ladies of the city.

This *sign* was hard to miss, but apparently not many cowhands could read. Five people were shot to death the year we arrived.

LUMBER

EAT

CANVAS

DODGE SALOON

AMUSEMENT PARLOR

SALOON

HATS

LEATHER DUNGAREE & HEMP ROPE

TUBS

BARBER

THE CARRYING of FIREARMS STRICTLY FORBIDDEN

The *stockyards* held thousands of cattle waiting to ship out to Chicago and other points east. We left our herd there, and Grizzly collected a heap of money.

Dodge was home to *19 saloons,* which is one for every 60 of its citizens.

LEDGER	June–September 1878
BEGINNING BALANCE	$3.25
INCOME	
4 months' wages	$120
EXPENSES	
hat	$20
pants	$12
shirt	$8
boots	$25
cut and shave	$1
Great Western Hotel (2 nights room and board)	$24
CURRENT BALANCE	$33.25

Dodge City Is Seized
by a Fear of Indians

THE DRIVE WAS OVER, and I was considering my next move when all hell broke loose. It started with a band of cowboys from the Driscoll ranch, a day's ride south of Dodge. They came a-thundering down Front Street squawking about an army of renegade Indians that was headed north stealing horses and killing cattle. Turns out our old friends the Cheyenne had finally had their fill of bad beef and reservation life. More than 300 of them struck out for their old hunting grounds with a few companies of soldiers on their tail. For a week they had been moving north, trying to buy horses as they traveled. They were met by ranchers waving rifles, and a few people, white and red alike, got shot.

A day after the Driscoll cowboys arrived, Dodge was crawling with farmers, all taking refuge from the Indians. About 50 cowhands formed a posse to hunt the Cheyenne. Billy joined up and wanted me to set out with him. I believe he wanted a Cheyenne scalp to make up for the pride he lost on the trail. But I didn't see much point in chasing a bunch of homesick Indians, so I decided to stay behind.

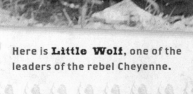

Here is **Little Wolf**, one of the leaders of the rebel Cheyenne.

Sad to say, those Cheyenne were chasing the past. They could still remember when the buffalo ran thick as prairie grass in Nebraska, Wyoming, and the Dakotas.

Soon after the white man arrived in these parts, the prairie was **crawling with hunters.** A man who was good with a rifle could make **$100 a day** collecting hides.

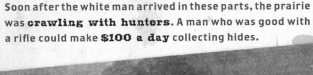

Not long before we arrived, men like **Charles Rath** (above) were shipping a quarter of a million buffalo hides out of Dodge every year. By 1878, there was nothing left to hunt but skeletons. Traders paid $8 a ton for scavenged bones and shipped them east to be made into fertilizer or bone china.

I Get an Accounting
and Some Hard Advice

WHILE WE AWAITED WORD from Billy and the rest of the Indian fighters, I set down to do some hard thinking on a weighty matter. After a year of dusty labor and little sleep I had a worn-out horse, a sore backside, and $33 that was fast slipping through the rope burns on my fingers. With no capital to speak of, how was a cowboy with big dreams to realize his aim of amassing a considerable fortune?

Old Grizzly, who had grown fond of me on the trail, sat down to render me some assistance. He showed me his accounting for the drive, which I have reproduced here. Then he imparted this wisdom to me: "Gator," said he, "this life ain't got but a few years left in it. The nesters and the big ranchers are choking us with barbed wire. 'Fore long you'll be lucky to drive a steer two miles without getting its nose stuck in a fence. If they could find a way they'd fence in the air and charge you to breathe. Only cowboys left'll soon be stuck on ranches punching a clock. I like you son, and I'd hate to see you join a sinking ship. If I was you, I would find another means of employment."

Last year, there were so many **beeves** in Dodge that Grizzly couldn't sell a steer for half this price. He had to drive the entire herd back to the Running Rooster.

IN THE MONEY

HERE IS GRIZZLY'S ACCOUNTING FOR THE DRIVE. DO NOT BE FOOLED BY THE SIZE OF THE NUMBERS.

In '71 this number was barely enough to pay the cook's wages. The Red River flooded something fierce, and more than three-quarters of Shang's herd drowned.

Income

horses (110 @ $25 ea.)	$2,750
stock to Darlington Indian Agency (800 beeves @ $19 ea.)	$15,200
to Armour & Co., Chicago (2,000 beeves @ $33 ea.)	$66,000
to XIT Ranch, Wyoming	
2-year-olds (970 @ $24 ea.)	$23,280
yearlings (890 @ $16 ea.)	$14,240
calves (120 @ $12 ea.)	$1,440
Total	$122,910

Expenses

wages (4 months)	
foreman ($125/mo. plus $18 board)	$572
cook ($75/mo. plus $18 board)	$372
drivers (15 @ $30/mo. plus $18 board)	$2,880
horses (120 @ $40 ea.)	$4,800
wagon	$125
mules and harness	$400
stock	
3-year-olds (3,000 @ $18 ea.)	$54,000
2-year olds (1,000 @ $12 ea.)	$12,000
yearlings (1,000 @ $6 ea.)	$6,000
trail fees	
Texas border (4,900 @ 4 cents/head)	$196
rustler scamp fee (200 @ 50 cents/head)	$100
Kansas watering fee (4,600 @ 10 cents/head)	$460
Total	$81,905
Total Profit (Income less Expenses)	$41,005

This looks like a **fat raise** of money, but most of it goes to pay back loans Shang took to buy the ranch and get through the bad years.

We Try to
Make the Most
of Our Wanderings

I sought a job with the deputy marshall, **Mr. Wyatt Earp**, who was paid $100 a month and $2.50 for every arrest he made. He told me I was too green for such dangerous work.

NEED I SAY that after Grizzly's talk, life looked pretty dim for a time. The dreams I had ridden through my childhood now seemed as old and tired as Prince, who was nearly fit for the glue factory after four months on the trail. Billy returned from his fool's errand with nothing to show for his troubles but an irritable temper and a thirst for strong drink. He and Grizzly and Guts pulled for Texas, leaving me and Wichita Will in Dodge. The Cheyenne were soon hunted down and put on a reservation. With their brethren—the Sioux, the Kiowa, and the Pawnee—all rounded up, there was plenty of ranch land to be had in the northwest. But seeing as I had no money, buying a herd seemed even harder than trailing one. Besides, after eating dirt for four months and listening to Grizzly's prophecies, I had lost my appetite for beef.

Will and I spent a fair bit of time drifting together from one vocation to another before we found our calling. I will set down our wanderings here in order to lead the reader to the fulfillment of this tale.

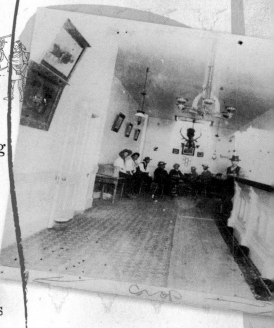

I put in cleaning up at the famous **Long Branch Saloon** for $6 a week but couldn't stand being under a roof that many hours a day.

We left Dodge in 1881 on a train to Chicago and put in at a meat-packing plant, but working with dead beeves proved to be more miserable than trailing live ones.

In Chicago, we scraped together admission fare to Buffalo Bill's show, *The Prairie Waif*, in which he employed five Indian chiefs and a maiden and put on a display of fancy rifle shooting of his own. Will insisted he could do better himself.

In 1882, Bill Cody put on a *grand Independence Day contest* in North Platte and advertised it with 5,000 handbills. It drew a thousand cowboys, and Will and I announced our presence by winning ribbons in shooting and bronco busting.

2d SILVER BENEFIT.

Opera House,
One Night Only.

Saturday Evening

THE ONLY AND ORIGINAL

BUFFALO BILL

HON. W. F. CODY,
Late Chief of the Scouts of the U. S. Army,

and his MAMMOTH COMBINATION
in his great Sensational Drama, entitled,

"The Prairie Waif,"

Introducing the Western Scout and Daring Rider,

Buck Taylor, King of the Cowboys.

A Genuine Band of Pawnee Indians,
Under Pawnee Billy, Boy Chief and Interpreter.

24 First Class Artists.   New and Beautiful Scenery

Mr. Cody, "Buffalo Bill," will give an exhibition of fancy Rifle Shooting,
holding his rifle in twenty different positions, in which he is acknowledged preeminent.

Prices of admission as usual.   Reserved seats, one dollar,
to be had at Forbes & Stromberg's.

BUFFALO BILL'S WILD WEST, OMAHA FAIRGROUNDS

MAY 19, 1883

We had *20 Pawnee braves* and their interpreter, Gordon William Lillie, who later took the name "Pawnee Bill."

For every show, we enacted "The Startling and Soul-Stirring Attack Upon the Deadwood Mail Coach," in which Bill arrived just in time to save the coach from the Pawnees.

At North Platte, Bill announced he was starting a new kind of show for an outdoor arena, and after our display on Independence Day he couldn't help but make us a part of it.

Here are the amazing *Wichita Will* and *Little John*, who could rope and ride the wildest buffalo that ever roamed the plains.

Here is *Captain A. H. Bogardus*, Champion Pigeon Shot of America. He saved thousands of real birds by inventing a clay "pigeon" target for shooting competitions.

Buck Taylor, King of the Cowboys, was as tall as me and could pick up a handkerchief from the ground while riding at top speed.

We Do Our
Roping and Riding
on Stage

THANKS TO BUFFALO BILL CODY, me and Wichita Will have lasted longer in the saddle than most of the cowhands we rode with in '78. I lost track of Grizzly and Guts and Billy, but the trail drive from Texas to parts north didn't survive more than another seven or eight years. Farmers put up so many barbed wire fences that you couldn't move a herd a mile without getting snagged on one. And after a while you didn't need to. Railroads were everywhere, and a Texas rancher could ship his beef to Chicago without setting foot or hoof on the trail.

I, for one, did not set foot on the trail again. But I am proud to say that I have spent 17 years on stage and fairground, making good money—$40 a week—and entertaining spell-bound audiences with feats of skill and daring. And though the great era of the cowboy has ended, I plan to keep the memory of it alive, as long as the people will come out for four hours of thrills and excitement, and are willing to dig into their pockets to do it.

Sitting Bull joined the show in **1885**. He made $50 a week and more for selling his autograph, but he gave most of it away to beggars. After four months of being gawked at he went back to the reservation to live with his people.

In **1893** we took on Russian cossacks, Argentinian gauchos, Turks, Arabs, Algerian Zouaves, and other colorful horsemen and called it the Congress of Rough Riders of the World.

BUFFALO BILL'S WILD WEST AND CONGRESS OF ROUGH RIDERS OF THE WORLD.

COL. W. F. CODY — LITTLE JOHN

THE BRAVE **COSSACKS** OF THE **CAUCASUS** IN WILD STRANGE FEATS AND FEARLESS EQUITATION.

We went to Europe for the first time in **1887** to play for **the queen**, taking with us more than 200 performers, 180 horses, 18 buffalo (almost as many as you could find in the wild at the time), 10 mules, 10 elk, 5 Texas steers, 4 donkeys, and 2 deer.

ᴅGER

1878–1900

ᴵNNING BALANCE:		$33.25
ᴼME:	Wild West Show	$40/week
	predicted book sales	$120,000
ᴾENSES:	fine living	$35/week
ᵁRRENT BALANCE:	varied investments (Armour & Co., Levi–Strauss & c.)	$128,600

WILL TELLS ME I THINK TOO MUCH OF MY FUTURE IN *THE WRITING BUSINESS.*

BUT I ALWAYS SAY

A MAN THAT THINKS SMALL LIVES SMALL.

Afterword
A. J. "Little John" Larken's Wild West
by Marc Aronson

HAVE YOU EVER READ one of those novels where you start to realize that what the narrator tells you is only half of the story? That's how Little John's account of his life on the Texas cattle drives strikes me. Neither Dr. Peter Blodgett of the Huntington Library nor I have been able to find any trace of Little John or the Larken family, yet so much of what Little John describes is exactly true. In fact, his story seems to be many true stories all rolled together.

The main story is about the great cattle drives of the 1860s and 1870s, when hard-riding, hard-living cowboys drove 5 million longhorns from Texas to the train depots of Kansas, where they were shipped on to the meat-packing plants of Chicago. Everything Little John tells us about how to ride, rope, and brand is accurate—as are his descriptions of the hard life of the cowhands. Shanghai Morse seems to resemble an actual cattle baron named Shanghai Pierce, a larger-than-life figure whose voice was said to be "too loud for indoor use." Pierce supposedly arrived in Texas with 75 cents in his pocket and died the millionaire owner of 200,000 acres of ranch land. Morse's ranch probably looked a lot like the drawing on pages 14-15.

Indeed Little John's drawings tell more even than his words—the crew on a Texas ranch was a mixed bunch. In the early days, two-thirds of the cowboys working the trail drives were Mexican or African American. In that regard, Little John's story is a lot more realistic than many popular novels and films in which blacks are invisible and Mexicans are sleepy sidekicks to energetic cowboys.

The problem of Westerns gets to the second big story Little John is telling us: how the actual West changed into the Wild West of our imaginations. As a kid, Little John probably knew the West from Ned Buntline's novels. Ned actually traveled briefly in the West and wrote dozens of popular novels about gunfighters, cowboys, and Indians. Little John, too, says he spent time as a cowhand, then went on to play one in Buffalo Bill's shows. The West really was like that—you might be out on the trail one day, then sailing off to Europe to play the part of a cowboy in a touring show the next. Take the Deadwood stage that appears in Little John's drawing of Buffalo Bill's show on pages 40-41. That very coach was actually used on the Deadwood-Cheyenne run and attacked by robbers. Buffalo Bill purchased it and staged the dramatic chase for paying audiences. And by the early 1900s the first Western movies featured their own versions of chases and robberies. So the West was a place of adventure and, at the very same moment, the setting for novels, plays, and soon movies all telling their own versions of those same escapades.

The third story that Little John tells is the clash between Indians and the new settlers of the West. That saga has often been portrayed as a battle between heroic cowboys and savage Indians. In truth it's a sad tale with few heroes on the side of the settlers. When the long drives began in 1866, the Indians still considered the Great Plains to be their hunting grounds. Every space that was made for cows, ranchers, railroads, or new towns squeezed the original Americans off their land. The escape from Indian Territory described by Little John—known as the Cheyenne Exodus—was a last-ditch attempt by the Cheyenne people to recover their old way of life. By the 1880s, all the Great Plains people had been confined to reservations a fraction of the size of their original lands. If you take a map showing the advancing borders of new settlement, you could also reverse it and call it "the declining space for native nations." Whether you call the history of the West an advance or a retreat depends on which story you want to tell.

So there you have it: I can't find Little John himself in the history books, but I do see the places he visited, the things he claimed to have done, the Ned Buntline novels he said he read, and the Buffalo Bill shows he wants us to believe he starred in. Even the stories he half tells us—about the forced retreat of the Indians—were true. So what is the real heart of the story of the West? I think it is in us: We all want to imagine a time and place where a person with guts, will, and spirit could ride the range, fight off the bad guys, and make his own way. The story of the West is still thrilling because we want that chance to be a roughriding hero—whether on horseback or in our imagination.

List of Illustrations

These illustrations have been verified as historically authentic; copies can be found in museum collections and other reputable archives. Illustrations not listed here are attributed to Little John Larken, and, while they appear to be accurate, their historical authenticity cannot be verified.

Further Reading

There are a great many books on library shelves that offer readers a way to read more about the people, places, and events Little John describes. Rather than making a list as long and sloppy as a herd of cattle, we've picked out examples of some of the interesting approaches authors have taken.

COWBOY LIFE

Axelrod, Alan. Songs of the Wild West. Metropolitan Museum of Art, 1991.

Christian, Mary Blount. Hats Are for Watering Horses: Why the Cowboy Dressed That Way. Hendrick-Long, 1994.

Ichord, Loretta. Skillet Bread, Sourdough, and Vinegar Pie: Cooking in Pioneer Days. Millbrook, 2003.

Schanzer, Rosalyn. The Old Chisholm Trail: A Cowboy Song. National Geographic, 2001.

Editors of Time-Life Books. The Cowboys. Time-Life Books, 1973.

AFRICAN AMERICANS AND VAQUEROS IN THE WEST

Freedman, Russell. In The Days of The Vaqueros: America's First True Cowboys. Clarion Books, 2001.

Katz, William Loren. Black People Who Made the Old West. Africa World Press, 1992.

Sandler, Martin. Vaqueros: America's First Cowmen. Henry Holt and Co., 2001.

NATIVE PEOPLES

Bial, Raymond. The Cheyenne (Lifeways series). Benchmark, 2001.

Roop, Peter and Connie. Sitting Bull. Scholastic, 2002.

BUFFALO BILL'S WILD WEST

Alter, Judy. Wild West Shows: Rough Riders and Sure Shots. Franklin Watts, 1997.

Spies, Karen Bornemann. Buffalo Bill Cody: Western Legend. Enslow, 1998.

LAWMEN

Green, Carl R., and William R. Sandford. Wyatt Earp (Outlaws and Lawmen of the Wild West series). Enslow, 2009.

ONLINE RESOURCES

Hosted by the Library of Congress, this gallery of photographs from the collection of the Denver Public Library covers the history of the American West, 1860-1920:

http://memory.loc.gov/ammem/award97/codhtml/hawphome.html

Although part of the Buffalo Bill Historical Center, the McCracken Research Library Digital Collection includes images not just of Buffalo Bill but also Plains Indians and the art of the West.

http://www.bbhc.org/hmrl/collection.cfm

Encyclopedia

In which unusual words are defined and additional information is offered about historical figures and places mentioned in the text.

BARBED WIRE: Wire with sharp points on it that was patented in 1874. It quickly became popular for those who wanted to fence in their land—and hated by those who wanted open range for grazing cattle. See pages 36 and 42.

BLACK HILLS WAR: One of the last in a series of wars between the Indians and the U.S. Army. In the 1850s, farmers and ranchers began to settle across the Great Plains, claiming land long inhabited by the Sioux, Cheyenne, and Arapaho Indians. Conflicts over territory led to several wars. By the time the Black Hills War ended, in 1877, the people who had once hunted freely all across the Plains were confined to small reservations in Indian Territory and the Dakotas. See pages 12-13.

NED BUNTLINE (1813–1886): A pseudonym of E. Z. C. Judson, who was for a time the most popular writer in America. He wrote action-packed books set on the sea or in the West. He was the first to include Buffalo Bill in a story and wrote the play that first got Bill onto the stage. See page 44.

SOLOMON D. BUTCHER (1856–1927): Photographer who lugged his heavy camera to take some 4,000 images of the pioneers in Nebraska. See photographs on pages 30-31.

CHEYENNE EXODUS: Attempt by the Northern Cheyenne to flee their reservation in Indian Territory and return to their hunting grounds. The Cheyenne had been forced out of the Dakotas in 1877 after the Black Hills War. But conditions in Indian Territory were so terrible that more than 300 men, women, and children fled back to the north. Though some of the escaping Northern Cheyenne were captured and surrendered, a group led by Little Wolf managed to reach their homeland in Montana. See pages 34, 38, and 44.

CHISHOLM TRAIL: One of several cattle trails that linked Texas ranches to the northern railroads. Just after the Civil War, Texas cattleman Joseph McCoy realized that there needed to be a safe, easy path to herd longhorns to the railroad. He set up pens to hold cows at Abilene, Kansas, next to the railroad, and marked a trail down to Texas, via Jesse Chisholm's trading post. See page 9.

WILLIAM F. CODY, AKA BUFFALO BILL (1846–1917): Scout turned showman who brought the Wild West to the world. A Pony Express rider at 15, a buffalo

hunter for the railroad, a scout for the army, Bill lived an adventurous life. Then, after meeting Ned Buntline, he began to tell that story on stage. The Wild West extravaganza he created was a great success and had fans all over the planet. See pages 6, 7, 24, 27, 39, 40-41, 42, 43, 44, 45.

GEORGE ARMSTRONG CUSTER (1839–1876): A born soldier who lived to fight. Custer won a string of battles fighting for the Union in the Civil War. But after the war he was court-martialed when he left his post to visit his wife. Needing to prove his worth, he massacred Cheyenne (mainly women and children) in 1868. In 1876, during the Black Hills War, he led his men to disaster at the Battle of Little Big Horn, where he lost his life. See page 13.

DIME NOVEL: The name given to the paperback books that publishers, starting in 1860, began selling for the low price of a nickel or a dime. All of the books featured strong heroes, dastardly villains, and thrilling battles. Many were set in the Wild West. By 1895, cheap magazines took the place of these inexpensive books. See pages 15 and 44.

WYATT EARP (1848–1929): U.S. marshal and sharpshooter who served as a lawman in Dodge City off and on from 1875 to 1878. He fought in the famous 1881 gunfight at the OK Corral in Tombstone, Arizona. See pages 38 and 45.

INDIAN TERRITORY: The land allotted in 1831 by the U.S. government to the Five "Civilized" Tribes. These tribes had originally lived in the Southeast and were forced to leave their homes and move west. At first they were granted lands covering part of what is now Arkansas and Oklahoma, then just Oklahoma, then just the eastern half of the region. In the 1870s, many of the Indians of the Great Plains were forced to move to the shrinking Indian Territory. When Oklahoma became a state in 1907, there was no longer any separate Indian Territory. See pages 9, 12, 20, 24, 31, and 44.

LITTLE WOLF, AKA LITTLE COYOTE (CA 1820–1904): A leader of the Northern Cheyenne during the Cheyenne Exodus. In 1878, faced with terrible conditions in Indian Territory, Little Wolf and Dull Knife led 300 Cheyenne back to their homelands in Montana. While Dull Knife's group was caught, Little Wolf's people reached Montana where their descendants remain today. See pages 25 and 34.

LONGHORN: Breed of cattle with distinctive horns. The Spanish brought cows to the New World, and some of those cattle escaped and roamed on their own. These cows had unusually long horns—up to seven feet from tip to tip—and could live on brush or weeds. See pages 16, 44, and 45.

MUSTANG: Feral, or wild, horse. Some horses brought to America by the Spanish escaped, finding food for themselves. Indians, and later ranchers, often tried to catch the descendants of those feral horses, but some still roam free to this day and are protected by the government. See pages 10, 14-15, 16, 17, and 20.

SITTING BULL (1834–1890): A leader of the Hunkpapa Sioux, who helped defeat General Custer at Little Big Horn and continued to urge his people to resist the government. He eventually surrendered and later appeared in Buffalo Bill's Wild West show. See pages 13, 42, and 45.

SOD HOUSE: Home built from rectangles of earth held together by thick roots. In 1862, the government offered free land to anyone who started a farm in certain states and cultivated the soil for five years. To build homes where there was little wood, homesteaders used sod. These houses kept cool in the summer and warm in the winter. But they also allowed insects to thrive. See pages 30-31.

TRANSCONTINENTAL RAILWAY: The first coast-to-coast train network, completed in May 1869 when the Union Pacific and the Central Pacific railroad tracks were linked. Now goods (like the meat packed in Cedar Rapids factories) could find their way from factories to stores around the country. See pages 6-7.

WINCHESTER: Rifle that could be shot and shot again without having to reload; often called "the gun that won the West." See page 24.

Thank you to Joan Wells of the North Fort Worth Historical Society and Tara Marsh of Brucemore, Inc., for helping us with our photo research; to Dr. Peter Blodgett for insight into this history; to Allen Barra for sharing books, lore, and his Ned Buntline novels; and to Jane Folger of Maplewood Memorial Library for, once again, compiling an excellent list of further readings.

A BOOK BY ARONSON & GLENN LLC AND TOD OLSON LLC
Produced by Marc Aronson, John W. Glenn, and Tod Olson
Text by Tod Olson
Book design, art direction, and production by Jon Glick, mouse + tiger
Illustrations by Scott Allred and Gregory Proch
Copyediting by Sharon Brinkman

Published by the National Geographic Society
John M. Fahey, Jr., *President and Chief Executive Officer*
Gilbert M. Grosvenor, *Chairman of the Board*
Tim T. Kelly, President, *Global Media Group*
John Q. Griffin, *Executive Vice President; President, Publishing*
Nina D. Hoffman, *Executive Vice President; President, Book Publishing Group*
Melina Gerosa Bellows, *Executive Vice President, Children's Publishing*

Prepared by the Book Division
Nancy Laties Feresten, Vice President, Editor in Chief, Children's Books
Jonathan Halling, *Design Director, Children's Publishing*
Jennifer Emmett, *Executive Editor, Children's Books*
Carl Mehler, *Director of Maps*
R. Gary Colbert, *Production Director*
Jennifer A. Thornton, *Managing Editor*

Staff for This Book
Jennifer Emmett, *Project Editor*
Eva Absher, *Art Director*
Lori Epstein, *Illustrations Editor*
Grace Hill, *Associate Managing Editor*
Lewis R. Bassford, *Production Manager*
Susan Borke, *Legal and Business Affairs*

Manufacturing and Quality Management
Christopher A. Liedel, *Chief Financial Officer*
Phillip L. Schlosser, *Vice President*
Chris Brown, *Technical Director*
Nicole Elliott, *Manager*
Rachel Faulise, *Manager*

Photography and Illustrations Credits
Abbreviations:
SA = illustration by Scott Allred
JG = illustration by Jon Glick, mouse + tiger
GP = illustrations(s) by Gregory Proch
LOC = courtesy The Library of Congress
t = top, c = center, b = bottom, l = left, r = right

Front cover (c) and spine (b): SA; front cover (tl, tr, back flap): GP; back cover (tl, cl, bl, background): LOC; back cover (tr): GP

Pages 1 (tl, tr): GP; 1 (b): LOC; 3: GP; 6 (l): GP; 6 (r): LOC; 7 (t): LOC; 7 (c): image courtesy of Brucemore; 7 (b): GP; 8 (bl): GP; 8 (tr, cr): LOC; 8 (br): courtesy Peter Newark American Pictures/The Bridgeman Art Library (PNP 244856); 9: JG; 10 (l): GP; 10-11: GP; 12 (bl): GP; 12 (br): LOC; 13 (tl, cr): LOC; 13 (bl): GP; 14-15: SA; 16 (l) and 17 (all): GP; 18 (all): GP; 19 (t): LOC; 19 (b): courtesy Peter Newark American Pictures/The Bridgeman Art Library (PNP 245424); 20 (l): GP; 20 (br): courtesy Denver Public Library; 21 (t, b): LOC; 20 (c): JG; 22 (all): GP; 23 (t): courtesy the North Fort Worth Historical Society, Forth Worth, Texas (P2009.1178); 23 (br): JG; 24 (l): GP; 24 (tr): courtesy Peter Newark American Pictures/The Bridgeman Art Library (PNP 247820); 24-25 (b): LOC; 25 (t): courtesy the National Archives; 25 (c): GP; 26-27: SA; 28 (bl, tr): GP; 29 (tr): JG; 29 (b): LOC; 30 (br): GP; 30-31 (t): courtesy Nebraska State Historical Society (RG2608-1784); 31 (b): courtesy Nebraska State Historical Society (RG2608-2430); 31 (br): JG; 32-33: SA; 34 (bl): GP; 34 (br): LOC; 35 (t): © Butler Institute of American Art, Youngstown, OH, USA/The Bridgeman Art Library (BIA 327366); 35 (cl): courtesy Kansas Historical Society;

35 (br): Public Domain; 36-37 (all): GP; 38 (l): GP; 38 (t): courtesy Allen Barra; 38 (b): courtesy Kansas Historical Society; 39 (tl): courtesy Archives Charmet/The Bridgeman Art Library (CHT 189398); 39 (tr): courtesy Denver Public Library; 39 (b): GP; 40-41: SA; 42 (bl): GP; 42 (br): LOC; 43 (t): Public Domain; 43 (r): LOC; 46 (l): courtesy Allen Barra; 46 (r): LOC; 47: LOC.

The National Geographic Society is one of the world's largest nonprofit scientific and educational organizations. Founded in 1888 to "increase and diffuse geographic knowledge," the Society works to inspire people to care about the planet. It reaches more than 325 million people worldwide each month through its official journal, *National Geographic*, and other magazines; National Geographic Channel; television documentaries; music; radio; films; books; DVDs; maps; exhibitions; school publishing programs; interactive media; and merchandise. National Geographic has funded more than 9,000 scientific research, conservation and exploration projects and supports an education program combating geographic illiteracy. For more information, visit nationalgeographic.com.

For more information, please call 1-800-NGS LINE (647-5463) or write to the following address:
National Geographic Society
1145 17th Street N.W.
Washington, D.C. 20036-4688 U.S.A.

Visit us online at www.nationalgeographic.com/books

For librarians and teachers: www.ngchildrensbooks.org

More for kids from National Geographic: kids.nationalgeographic.com

For information about special discounts for bulk purchases, please contact National Geographic Books Special Sales: ngspecsales@ngs.org

For rights or permissions inquiries, please contact National Geographic Books Subsidiary Rights: ngbookrights@ngs.org

Library of Congress Cataloging-in-Publication Data

Olson, Tod.
 How to get rich on a Texas cattle drive : in which I tell the honest truth about rampaging rustlers, stampeding steers, and other fateful hazards on the wild Chisholm Trail / by Tod Olson ; illustrated by Scott Allred and Gregory Proch.
   p. cm.
 ISBN 978-1-4263-0524-5 (hardcover : alk. paper) -- ISBN 978-1-4263-0525-2 (library binding : alk. paper)
1. Chisholm Trail--Juvenile literature. 2. Cattle trails--West (U.S.)--History--19th century--Juvenile literature. 3. Cattle drives--West (U.S.)--History--19th century--Juvenile literature. 4. Frontier and pioneer life--West (U.S.)--Juvenile literature. 5. West (U.S.)--History--19th century--Juvenile literature. I. Allred, Scott. II. Proch, Gregory. III. Title.
 F596.O62 2010
 978'.02--dc22
                          2009040442
Printed in U.S.A.

10/WOR/1